Disney Cinderella

Read-Along
STORYBOOK AND CD

This is the story of *Cinderella*. You can read along with me in your book. You will know it is time to turn the page when you hear the Fairy Godmother wave her magic wand like this. . . .

Let's begin now.

For information address Disney Press, 1101 Flower Street, Glendale, California 91201.
Printed in China
First Box Set Edition, May 2017   10 9 8 7 6 5 4 3 2 1
FAC-025393-17034
ISBN 978-1-368-00755-9

For more Disney Press fun, visit www.disneybooks.com

Disney PRESS

Los Angeles • New York

Once there was a kind and beautiful girl named Cinderella, who lived with her cruel stepmother and two selfish stepsisters, Anastasia and Drizella.

Every morning, Cinderella told her little mice and bird friends about her dreams. "They're wishes my heart makes when I'm asleep. If I believe in them, someday they'll come true!"

Then one day an announcement arrived from the palace. "The King is giving a royal ball in honor of the Prince. Every maiden in the kingdom is commanded to come!"

The stepsisters were thrilled, and so was Cinderella. "Every maiden! That means I can go, too!"

Her stepsisters laughed, but her stepmother smiled slyly. "You may go, Cinderella, if you do all your work. And if you find something suitable to wear!"

All that day, Cinderella's stepmother and stepsisters shouted orders at her. Cinderella's mice and bird friends watched sadly. "Poor Cinderelly. They keeping her so busy she never get her dress done."

Then they had an idea! "We can do it!" Soon, they were happily snipping and stitching to make a lovely dress for Cinderella.

When evening came, tired Cinderella trudged up the stairs to her tiny attic room.

When she saw the pretty gown they had made for her, Cinderella could hardly speak. "Oh! How can I ever… oh, thank you so much!"

Dressed and ready, Cinderella ran downstairs. "Wait! Please! Wait for me!"

Anastasia and Drizella saw how lovely Cinderella looked and flew into a jealous rage. They ripped her dress to shreds.

"That's enough, girls," Lady Tremaine said at last. "Don't upset yourselves before the ball. It's time to go."

Laughing cruelly, they left.

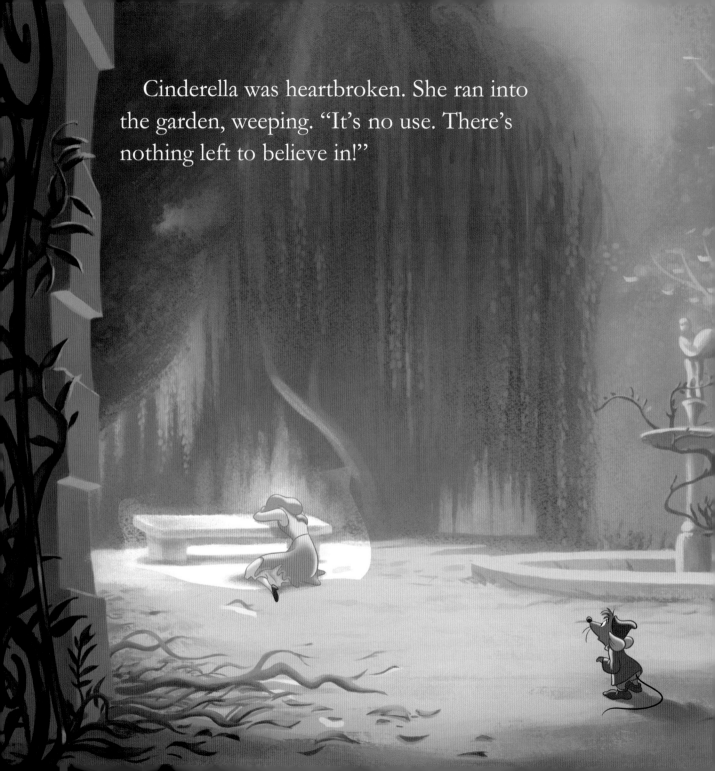

Cinderella was heartbroken. She ran into the garden, weeping. "It's no use. There's nothing left to believe in!"

Suddenly, she heard a cheery voice. "Nonsense, child. If you didn't believe, I wouldn't be here ... and here I am!"

Cinderella looked up and saw an older woman smiling at her. "I'm your Fairy Godmother. Dry your tears. We must hurry!"

"First we need a pumpkin and some mice. Now for the magic words: bibbidi-bobbidi-boo!" With a wave of her wand, the Fairy Godmother turned the pumpkin into a coach and the mice into white horses.

The Fairy Godmother hurried Cinderella to her coach. "But . . . but . . . my dress."

"Yes, yes . . . it's lovely—good heavens, child! You can't go in that. You need a dress. Well, just leave it to me. What a gown this will be! Bibbidi-bobbidi-boo!"

The Fairy Godmother waved her wand, and
Cinderella's rags changed into a shimmering gown.
On her feet, two dainty glass slippers twinkled
like stars.

"Oh, it's like a wonderful
dream come true!"

But the Fairy Godmother gave Cinderella a
warning. "On the stroke of twelve, the spell will
be broken and everything will be as it was before."
Cinderella blew the Fairy Godmother a kiss,
and the coach sped away toward the castle.

Meanwhile, at the ball, the Grand Duke and the King watched the Prince greet one maiden after another with a polite but bored expression.

Then, suddenly, a hush fell over the ballroom.

The Prince looked toward the grand entrance. A lovely girl in a dress the color of moonlight stood there with all eyes on her. It was Cinderella, but her stepmother and stepsisters didn't recognize her. "Who is she, Mother?"

"I don't know, but she seems familiar."

Prince Charming knew he'd found the girl of his dreams. "May I have this dance?" As the music played, they waltzed around the ballroom and out into the garden. Soon enough, the castle clock began to chime.

"Oh, my goodness! It's midnight! I must go! Good-bye!"

As Cinderella ran away, the Prince rushed after her. "Wait! Come back! I don't even know your name!"

Cinderella darted through the ballroom and raced down the palace steps, losing a glass slipper on the way. The clock chimed on.

Cinderella jumped into her coach and sped away.
Suddenly, the spell was broken. The coach
became a pumpkin, the horses turned back into
mice, and Cinderella was again dressed in rags.

The next day, the King sent out a royal proclamation. "Every maiden in the kingdom must try on the glass slipper. And the girl whose foot fits, will wed the Prince."

Cinderella couldn't hide her happiness from her stepmother. "So, Cinderella is the girl the Prince seeks. Well, he'll never find her!" And with that, she locked Cinderella in her attic room.

"Please! You can't do this! Please, let me out!"

But the Stepmother ignored Cinderella's cries.

Before long, the Grand Duke and a royal footman arrived with the glass slipper. The Stepmother and stepsisters smiled their sweetest smiles and ushered them in. Both Anastasia and Drizella were eager to find some way to get their feet to fit the slipper!

But though they pushed and shoved, neither of the stepsisters could squeeze a foot into it. "I don't understand why! It always fit perfectly before!"

Meanwhile, Cinderella's mice friends struggled to get the key out of the Stepmother's pocket without her noticing.
Then they had to lug it all the way upstairs to the attic. "Thissa way. Up, up, up wif it. Gotta hurry!" They slid it beneath Cinderella's door. She was free!

Downstairs, the Grand Duke knew neither stepsister was the girl he sought. "Are there any other maidens in the household?"

"There is no one else, Your Grace."

Just as he turned to leave, Cinderella ran downstairs. "Your Grace! Your Grace! May I try it on?"

As the footman carried the slipper to Cinderella, the Stepmother tripped him, and he fell! The slipper smashed into a hundred pieces. The Grand Duke was horrified!

Cinderella smiled and reached into her pocket. "Perhaps I can help. You see, I have the other slipper."

The Stepmother and stepsisters gasped. With a low bow, the Grand Duke slipped it onto Cinderella's dainty foot. It fit perfectly!

Soon wedding bells rang throughout the kingdom. As the happily married couple rode away in the royal coach, Cinderella realized she had been right, after all. If you keep on believing, your dreams will come true.

And so, they all lived happily ever after.